THE RIPPLE TANK EXPERIMENT

JEAN BLEAKNEY

LAGAN PRESS
BELFAST
1999

Acknowledgements

Some of these poems have previously appeared in *Books Ireland, Brangle, Poetry Ireland Review, The Rialto, Up the Hill* (Harmony Hill Writers Group), *Verse, Women's Work VII&VIII, Women's News*; or have been broadcast on BBC Radio Ulster.

Published by
Lagan Press
7 Lower Crescent
Belfast
BT7 1NR

© Jean Bleakney

The moral right of the author has been asserted.

ISBN: 1 873687 52 4
Author: Bleakney, Jean
Title: The Ripple Tank Experiment
1999

Cover Design: Kevin Cushnahan
Set in Palatino
Printed by Noel Murphy Printing, Belfast

for Paul, Stephen and Katherine
　　—with love

Jean Bleakney was born in Newry, Co. Down in 1956. She was educated at Queen's University, Belfast. A former biochemist, she currently works in a garden centre in Belfast.

THE RIPPLE TANK EXPERIMENT

Contents

Breaking the Surface	13
By Starlight on Narin Strand	14
Letters from Cyprus	16
The Sanderlings	19
Holiday Poetry	20
Depending on the Angle	21
Nightscapes	22
Confessions of a Gardener	23
Be Careful of the Lilies!	24
Ménage à Trois	25
In Praise of Cinquefoils	26
The Valentine Rose	27
A Rose By Any Other ...	28
Whenever	29
On Circumvention	30
Who Goes There?	31
Out to Tender	32
In Memoriam	33
Primordium	34
Equinoctial Imperatives	35
Mock Orange	36
Postcard	37
Black and White	38
The View From Carran West	39
The Physics of a Marriage	40
Life on the Fault Line	41
A Woman of Our Times	42
How Can You Say That?	43
Stargazing for Feminists	44
Dick Detail	45
Mid-Cycle	46
Fidelity, Fidelity	47
Every Little Helps	48
Afterwards	49
Round About Christmas Eve	50

Winter Revisions	*51*
Spring	*52*
Backspin	*53*
Knitting	*54*
Lines	*56*
Shoreline	*57*
Summer love was ever thus ...	*58*
The Unreliable Narrator	*59*
Dangerous Driving	*60*
A Little Knowledge	*62*
Why?	*63*
Fuchsia *magellanica*	*64*
Always	*65*
On Going Without Saying	*66*
At a Bend in the Road	*67*
A Watery City	*68*
A Windless Night in June, There Being No Stars	*70*

BREAKING THE SURFACE

I have gone beyond the childish delight
of plumping the heaviest stone
into the shallows, and yet,
distance throwing has defeated me.

Head bowed, I clamber the scree of the shore
filling my pockets with its loose change
—each cool button of basalt
tentatively flipped before selection.

This is my talent—a whiplash from the hip,
the skite, innumerable tangents, then a glide
until, as if remembering the laws of gravity,
it stops and languidly slews before anchoring.

One facet of the art of skimming, I say
is that, by overriding the big splash,
sound release is reduced to a whispering skiff
thus reinforcing the attenuated decay of energy ...

I take it, from your broadening grin,
that no amount of gilding with applied physics
can disguise pure panache *or* my primitive desire
to rearrange the shoreline—in a minimalist sort of way.

BY STARLIGHT ON NARIN STRAND

On a hot summer night, heavy with stars,
I am standing on the beach, stiff-necked,
watching for Perseids which, depending
on their size and angle of impact,
skate long tangents of brightness
or disintegrate in a short broad fizz of light.

During the gaps between Perseids, I think
of Claudius Ptolemaeus, The Geographer
who, having mapped the ancient world,
tired of latitude and longitude and turned instead
to the wheels-within-wheels of the planets
and the fixed sphere of stars;

and how, noting the positions and magnitudes
of one thousand and twenty-eight stars,
he reached back across three millennia
to Babylon for the *Scorpion* and the *Bull*;
and humbly kept faith with the gods
in his naming of forty-eight constellations.

What pitch of darkness did he find
for such geometries? Did he travel,
by merchant ship to Ephesus or Antioch,
in order to pare down the horizon
and escape those mirrored fires—
the beams of the lighthouse at Alexandria?

Was he haunted by the frailty of night-vision
—how, when viewed directly, even the brightest star
diminishes? Did he think it mere illusion
or a god's conceit that leaves us trapped
like eternal nightwatchmen constantly scanning
the between-blackness of starlight?

This is what I am thinking about
at the hottest August of the century
on the darkest edge of the continent
as, during the intervals between Perseids
and the afterglow of spent wishes,
I faithfully retrace Ptolemy's dot-to-dot.

LETTERS FROM CYPRUS

I
The Wild Flowers of Spring

Who's the blow-in here, I wonder,
the spoiler in this contretemps of yellows?
Golden Crown Daisies and lemony Oxalis
are juxtaposed—in drifts, not intermingling.
Near neighbours on the colour wheel,
these hues are just too close for comfort.
Weeks from now, they'll frizzle back
to limestone. So what does it matter—as if
'indigenous' means anything out here (or anywhere)?
There will be photographs of course, although
development will mask such local subtleties.
Back home, the viewers will record
a daffodilic blur—a worthy foil
for the upper cobalt band, and the indiscriminate
blood-red spattering. They'll simply say
Look at the blue sky and those beautiful poppies!

II
Reading a Poet on Potamos Beach

Here, on this calico of crushed shells,
I can't decide if it's the shadowless height of the sun,
or the floating heat, or the heady sweetness of mimosa
that lifts this poem, heartwards, off the page.

Suddenly it seems as perfect and miraculous
as these microscopic minarets I'm sifting from the sand,
translucence-thin, each with its own notation
—the loveliest, a tapering spiral of maroon serifs.

Or, glimpsing now a far-off tanker
slowly trading blue horizons, is it distance?

It's almost as though, forty lines of longitude
from home, I'm arm-in-arm with a poet
who's dazzled by the sun and wondering
where on earth she left her heart.

III
At the Birthplace of Aphrodite

It's nothing like the Botticelli
here at Petra tou Romiou
although the distance view
of sea and sky approximates, it's barely
recognisable. He's missed so much.
He hasn't even shown
those thrusting hunks of limestone.
I suppose he was a touch
distracted by Her Ladyship.
And who could blame him.
But now each pilgrim
thirsting for a sip
of *actualité*
must reinvent the scene.

From cool clear aquamarine
a heavenly castaway
just happened on this sun-baked rocky shore.
(Let's not dwell
on that extremely improbable shell)
Scantily clad, she was, with little more
than flowing spray-soaked hair ...
Hold on. That's Dr. No!
and not a stones throw
from Baywatch. Stop right there!

Let's think instead of why *this* beach
with its elaborate geology

of smooth flat stones ... or maybe ...
now, this is probably pure kitsch,
but was it like a kind of training ground? Was that her angle—
to put every roughly anatomical-
(think heart-, think breast-, think testicle-)
shaped piece of hardcore through the mangle?
Could *anyone* be so career-driven?
Or did she,
Aphrodite,
simply *know* that this was skimmer's heaven?

IV
Heart-Stones

Sun-worshipping's a penance
on this unforgiving shingle,
and I'm no swimmer. What is there to do,
when shoulder-sore from skimming,
but look for heart-shaped stones
—those two-dimensional valentines, trophies
for the dearly-loved back home.

Yes, that's the one for her.
She'd like the quartzite veining.
She'd certainly appreciate
the shattered-glued-together look.

And having filled my pockets, even then,
I risk that steep slithery grind
back down to the waterline
to lift a little fist of rock,
the colour of hung meat, rough-flaked
like cross-cut muscle—a stone that is,
for all the world, a flayed heart.

Petra tou Romiou, Cyprus

THE SANDERLINGS
at Tramore Beach, Rosbeg

Consummate paddlers,
they vacillate (or so it seems)
between the pianissimo wavelets
and the dizzying drainings of waves.
How do they keep their balance?

Always out-running the breakers.
Always maintaining a shrewd remove
from loopy dogs and camera-toting tourists
who stop and gape (the dogs keep running)
at their sudden, choreographed departures.

Earthed again, they sieve
the gritty shallows; jittery, myopic,
as if attuned—as if extrapolating
danger from lifeless shells;
from gulls and crabs, grotesque in death.

Here—half-desert, half-flood-plain,
grave of the *Duquesa Santa Ana**—
the sanderlings have somehow learned
to read the tide like a book,
like a biblical epic.

*Armada ship

HOLIDAY POETRY

After yet another neon sunset, I went
to Derry for the day—shorts and T-shirt
silted up with sand and holiday money.
There, in a second-hand bookshop, I found
The Best American Poetry 1991.
I placed the £4 bet without a second glance,
suddenly desperate to escape the city heat.
Tonight, sitting on the dunes above Tramore,
it seems churlish to deny the fantasy that:
scouring the beach for shells at low tide
I saw a bleached plastic drum, labelled
To Whom It May Concern. There being
not another soul in sight, I opened it
and found this book, edited by Mark Strand;
this book, the colours of sand and sky
with airy cover-painting entitled
Rooms by the Sea (artist, Edward Hopper).
Impossible not to imagine it adrift
somewhere off the eastern seaboard,
fighting the currents around Nova Scotia
and Connecticut; pitching for home
as far south as the Florida Keys
before encountering the Gulf Stream ...
Anyway, here it is, open at my feet
—its pages flapping in the tidal breeze.
Re-oxygenated. *Bishop*-ish. Ultramarine.

DEPENDING ON THE ANGLE

Face down on the beach, head askew, the view
is stratified. It thins to bedded strand,
a vein of blue and squamous islands.
Bathers, paddlers, plodders
are corpuscular and slow.
They tow a line that slacks
to aimlessness. The heat
refracts and blurs.
The world is slight,
so light it might evaporate.
We cling together, sand and I.
My saline drip, drip, drip revives it.
I'm dissolving in this sweet syncytium.
I close my eyes and *dive* to beach-dreams.

    syncytium, (biol) a multinucleate cell; a tissue without distinguishable cell walls. [Greek, *syn*, together, *kytos*, vessel.]
—*The Chambers Dictionary*

NIGHTSCAPES

*If this was Donegal
I wouldn't be able to breathe
for fear of swallowing stars ...*

Tonight, summer thunderclouds
are bloomed sandstone pink
—city-lit to saturation;

etched with high silhouettes
—the fretwork of ash leaflets;
the blurred filigree of birch;

Lonicera *nitida* (Poor Man's Box)
—its swell of uncut hedge
could be a distant ancient forest.

Below the horizon of hedges,
beyond the quiescence of chromatophores
—a sudden symmetry of white.

I'm standing in a bowl of galaxies
with floating moons of Cosmos 'Purity'
and Magellanic Clouds of Artemesia.

In spangled panicles of privet
I count thirty-seven Pleiades
but not a single Pole Star.

Night moths are time-travellers
sampling a trillion vintages
of nectar, dusting aeons.

Here in the sub-night of cities
we shape our own mysteries;
cast our own constellations.

CONFESSIONS OF A GARDENER

I love the way a garden paints the seasons;
the perfect pitch of fragrances; the way
my tongue thrills to attenuated Latin.
I love all the between-finger-and-thumb bits
of sowing seeds and pinching out; I gently chart
the leaves of irises from base to tip
palpating each tumescence, coaxing flower.
I love the velvety caress of ripened anthers;
the way that pollen floods the whorls and loops
of fingertips—as sensual as sun on skin.

Sometimes, I specially select F1 Hybrids,
bred for uniformity and vigour, purely
to buck the odds by planting some in sunny pots
some in shady beds and some beneath the hedge.
At leisure, I enjoy spotting the difference.
I overwinter spring bulbs on the worktop
where they desiccate or sweat to blue fur.

My preferred *touch of drama* in the border
is not a sword-leaved phormium or palm
but rather a sapling, say a small apple tree,
being slowly throttled by bales of bindweed.
And occasionally in spring, I perform
a little murderously injudicious pruning.
For weeks I watch the unstaunchable sap.
It seeps, weeps, bleeds—depending on my mood—
perfect circles of blackness below each stump.

I content myself that there are certain things
a woman has to get out of her system somehow
and I'd really rather you knew—just in case
you'd got the wrong impression—just in case
you'd thought that it was all a bed of roses.

BE CAREFUL OF THE LILIES!

You'd think we'd know by now (Aren't these the days
of cheap Australian wine and huge bouquets?)

that pollen *stains*—not stains so much as sticks
with microscopic barbs. Burnt Orange flecks

indelible as scorch marks. Such a shame
whether it's cashmere or silk or denim.

The starchy buds are so innocuous
at first. Not like that other 'Look at Us!'

brigade. There are too many petals
on chrysanthemums—stiff as funerals.

Carnations are the same—a primped tableau.
It's as if lilies really want to grow

and multiply, the way they purse their lips;
then one by one each pupal bud unzips

to frisky stamens jostling in midair.
They seem to manage this when no-one's there

so that, opening the door on a room
askew with incense and lilies in full bloom,

how hard it is not to get intimate;
to resist doing something you might regret

in Burnt Sienna. They're out-and-out chancers,
those lilies, with their fulminant anthers.

MÉNAGE À TROIS

Today's the day. Two years I've been waiting
for a sniff of Rosa 'Seagull'; fretting
over all those shoots blanketed with greenfly
—flowerless shoots; shrugging at why,
instead of growing up through the Berberis
(Berberis *atropurpurea*, that is),
it had tilted off into the Fuchsia *magellanica*.
(Well, that's 'gardening' for ya!)

I'd imagined the flower pure white,
but so far, so butter-cream-with-a-slight-
warmth-of-peach. That was yesterday evening
—a bud fit to burst. I went to bed dreaming
the whole perfumery of roses,
daybreak-moist; the cool velvety closeness
of the petals. It was a bit of a shock
to look out and see a big brown blotch
centred on my one-and-only bloom: a bumblebee,
countersunk, as if it had died of ecstasy.

It hadn't. That was four hours ago.
Every now and then, a back leg moves: a slow
lazy stretch—a kind of smoothing-the-sheets
post-coital languor. How can I compete
with that? When I think of the tousled stamens;
the pollen from who-knows-where. It won't be the same.
I suppose it's Nature's way; and two's company ...
I know I should say *Take your time, Honey.*
This rose is big enough for both of us.
But it's so hard to be magnanimous
when you feel like shouting *Bugger off, Bee!*
Get your fat butt outta my reverie!

IN PRAISE OF CINQUEFOILS

He loves me, he loves me not ...
is such a convoluted plot.
How fickle petals are, how long
they sometimes take ... then get it wrong.

If time is short and love is true,
daisies aren't the flowers for you.
Take this botanical advice:
Buttercups are loaded dice.

THE VALENTINE ROSE

Whenever I unpeeled it, petal by petal
on a Blue Denmark dinner plate
—forty-three scarlet flakes, each
smaller than the one before, spiralling
inwards from the ribbed rim, homing in
on a golden frizz of immature stamens ...
the pattern it made—the sense
of perspective—was overwhelming.

Although it's open to interpretation,
this was not an act of vandalism,
not towards a bud already slack
as though its neck had been wrung.
Nor was I trying to explode a myth.
In retrospect, I prefer to think
I was breathing life into an old cliché.
Let's say I was making a meal of it.

A ROSE BY ANY OTHER ...
'Taxonomists have agreed to revert to using the name chrysanthemum.'
—*Gardening Which? November 1997*

Re-classifying Tricuspidaria *lanceolata*
as Crinodendron *hookerianum*
was no big deal.

It's only ever known as
the Lantern Tree (not to be confused
with Chinese Lantern, Physalis *alkekengii*).

Even Lithospermum's demise
—subsumed by Lithodora—
barely caused a ripple.

But then
(let's put it down
to pre-millennial cockiness)
those flower-crazed taxonomists
decided on Dendranthema ...
until, that is, appropriately in autumn,
some lover of words among them thought
Imagine a world with no chrysanthemums ...

WHENEVER

Whenever you've been
the length and breadth
of the straight and narrow;
when you're sick of clipped privet
and that *couldn't, wouldn't, shouldn't*
old refrain of the garden shears

—you gotta break out delta-wise.
Rip out the hedges. Cultivate
a whole new rubric. Try Amaranthus,
Oriental poppies, Liquidambar ... And while you're at it
practise saying *possible, palpable, lingual*
and other such vasodilatory words. Whenever.

ON CIRCUMVENTION

There's no time like the present ...
always arrives like a reprimand.
(Or maybe that's just me—long since
tethered to deferral.) I'm tense
about the here-and-now. I know
that I've neglected all my gardens.

Don't present me with the secateurs.
I'd turn away. But be assured
that if instead you coyly asked
Ever thought of cutting back the Lavatera?
I'd say *Many's the time, darlin'.*
Many's the time ...

WHO GOES THERE?

And having planted the purple Cotinus
and the variegated Pittosporum side by side,
in line with the bevelled glass door,
in line with the panelled hall
and the always-open kitchen door ...

Tangentially, they'll catch me when I'm
steeped in spuds or dishes; they'll flicker
in the corner of my green-accustomed eye.
That leafy congregration, especially backlit by sun,
will keep me on my toes the whole summer.

OUT TO TENDER
Ceasefire, 1994

All along the motorway
they're resurfacing and bridge-strengthening
and seeding the central reservation
with wild flowers.

But only an hour or so ahead
there is fierce growth in the ditches
and the road diminishes
to unmendable potholes.

And there are places where the light
suddenly drops; where the branches,
out of reach of the hedgecutter,
are irrevocably pleached.

***

The whole talk these days is about words;
the glitzy newly-honed nouns
—like *peace* and *process* and *permanence*.

But there are other things to be said
with reference to particular definitions
and in deference to the vernacular.

There are townlands where parameters
invariably decline to perimeters;
where you can't be middle-of-the-road
when you're the whole road.

Here come the cowboy landscapers
with their quick-fix Castlewellan Golds.
As an old Fermanagh woman would've said,
The same boys can do feats and shite wonders.

IN MEMORIAM

If it's over, *let it be over*,
how can we forget? We should not forget
the years that were rank with abscissions;
the days when our unuttered shame
was as stagnant as the cut flowers
blackening under cellophane;
the autumn when streets and townlands shrank
to funeral gatherings—as tightly concentric
as the petals of chrysanthemums;
the hopeless sense of everything falling away
except the leaves, the reddening leaves.

PRIMORDIUM

Last of all awakenings, the Ash
remains tight-lipped beyond Ascension Day.
Feigning death, it skews the season.
Even when the hard black bud scales have been cleaved,
they don't reflex and yield
but green to life, lengthening to talons
that cannot clasp those copper-tinted plumes,
yet cruelly teach *This is how the world is* ...

At leaf-drop, when the downward clatter echoes
under opaline October skies, there's wonder
at its long, long wintering.
Has heartwood held the memory of springs
that faltered under hailstones' icy flint?
Does it know of summers that never were?

EQUINOCTIAL IMPERATIVES
for Malachi O'Doherty

It's the precocity of spring that shocks
—alchemical forsythia;
a robin shadowing the garden fork;
the overnight extrusions on magnolia
like plump fledglings, wings reflexed, ready
for take-off. Why do we love *them* best of all
—even afterwards, weather-fretted?
Why do we lift a fleshy rust-tipped petal?

Boldest of all arrivals is the botanist
who eloquently puts us in the picture:
The situation with magnolia is this,
he says, as he delineates the flower ...
petals and sepals, being indistinguishable,
should be collectively addressed as tepals.

MOCK ORANGE
12th July 1998

As if it couldn't bear the weight of itself
—as if it were a glass of milk gone sour—
the double-flowered Philadelphus
has suddenly reneged on summer.

The tight-clipped lawns and patios of Ulster
are littered with rescinded petals
in overlapping clumps, like piecemeal shrouds.

POSTCARD
Sunday 16th August 1998

It's been the wettest summer here in years.
As suntans fade away and tourists leave,
we count the sun among the disappeared.

The seaside towns are stacked with souvenirs
that won't sell now. And still we can't believe
how bad it's been, the worst we've had in years

—no notion of a 'good day' perseveres.
We give the nod to autumn for reprieve
and count our hopes among the disappeared.

In rain that is commensurate with tears
another generation learns to grieve.
On this, the hardest summer here in years,
we count the maimed. We name the disappeared.

BLACK AND WHITE

Facing up to the truth of shooting stars
—that the earth is a whirling medieval flail,
making fire and dust of tiny remnant worlds—
is a terrible flicker
of how the black-and-white of things
can sometimes leave us inconsolable.

THE VIEW FROM CARRAN WEST

Only now, now that the leaves have fallen,
can we measure the season's growth
in lengths of bright untainted bark.

Only now, now that autumn's almost over,
can we see beyond to the deepening lough
where a summer sun rolled down the mountainside
to Inishtemple, Inishmean and Inisheher.

Except that now, now the view from the house
is opening up to winter, the mountain
has stolen the sun; the lough is blackening
and a storm from the west has set her heart
on littering the shore with broken branches.

THE PHYSICS OF A MARRIAGE

Well matched, they say of us. To me it's clear
that symmetry was just the half of it.
Same wavelength I suppose. Yes darling, we're
the ripple tank experiment that worked
and even though the floor got soaked
the pattern somehow held. We knew it would.
Those corrugations clinched. But oh the debt
to synchronicity and amplitude.

LIFE ON THE FAULT LINE

At the commencement of my fortieth year,
I am resolved to face up to electrolysis
and be more liberal with *Oil of Ulay*.
I am going to accept that equilibrium
depends on balances and cheques. I will
be more attentive to the lie of the land.
And in the certain knowledge that man
cannot survive on DIY and fly-tying,
I hereby give notice that my next poem
will be *The Aftershocks of Seismic Sex*
—an overlong epic centred on home ground.
Much research and doubtless much revision
will be required. It could take all year.
Now can I go to sleep?

A WOMAN OF OUR TIMES

I wish you wouldn't look at me
as if to say *It's a tip, this place.*
There must be six weeks' Sunday papers
on that sofa. You couldn't find room
to butter a slice of bread ...
you wouldn't want to put
a slice of bread on that worktop.
Would you ever consider hoovering?
I wish you'd think before you look.

I wish you'd BLINK instead and see
a Woman of Our Times
—a dedicated scientist
employing all of her resources
in the absence of outside funding
—a physicist painstakingly unravelling
the Second Law of Thermodynamics;
almost touching base in Chaos Theory
—a woman up to her eyes in entropy.

HOW CAN YOU SAY THAT?

I am your wife.
I can name and nurture
twenty-nine hardy geraniums.
I know that the secret of not ironing
is tumbling to the point
where gravity and steam
conjoin to creaselessness.
I know that cholesterol
gets a bad press considering
it is to sex hormones
what flour is to bread.
I think that low-salt
is also very suspect.
I know that in life,
there are no straight lines—
it's all angles and loops.
I know that colour
is the effluent of light;
that greenery is only thus
because reds and blues
are all a leaf desires.
On very windy nights
I am struck by the suddenness
of disappearing moonlight.
I have always thought
that infinity cuts both ways ...
I am *your* wife.
How can you say that my head
'is full of sweetie mice'?

STARGAZING FOR FEMINISTS

Well proud of the horizon,
undressed to kill, the both of them
—full moon all bosomy white
and Venus, faceted and glittery,
as bold as you like;
admiring one another
as well they might
and amplified because of it.

Between, caught up in the cross-talk,
Orion: Mighty Hunter, skirt-chaser,
tormentor of the Pleiades
—but not such a big lad tonight.
As body outlines go
he's a bit splayed out,
a bit of a John Doe,
now that the girls are back in town.

DICK DETAIL

To give is better ... doesn't always hold
especially when oral sex comes up.
The pleasure stakes are loaded. Sorry guys,
it doesn't help to think of chocolate *Chup-
a Chups*. Aside from girls who like to plough
an altogether softer bodyscape,
there's those among the straight-to-slightly-skewed
who'd rather lick a nipple into shape.

MID-CYCLE

You worry that I scarcely
think about you anymore;
that kids and plants and weight control
have undermined the score;

that daytime parting kisses
are perfunctory and pared;
that *Not tonight, love* grievances
are seldom ever aired.

But riding high on hormones,
I'm contemplating you
—my inhibitions melt away;
my thoughts are turning blue ...

I'm in a shopping centre
on a wet and windy night
to buy you *Head & Shoulders, Vick*
and *Durex Fetherlite*.

FIDELITY, FIDELITY

The ever-tilting monorail of love
demands a sense of balance. It can take
a weather eye and faith in gyroscopes
not to panic, not to pull the brake.

When never-met horizons steal the eye,
familiar stations blur. Desire deletes
embankments, viaducts and fallow fields.
The window mists with gathering deceits.

Get off the train. Discover the illusion
was parallax—the powerful undertow
that drains away the near-to-middle distance
but steadies skylines. Only then you'll know

how destinations often disappoint.
The view can pale. The sun might never shine.
Hearts are mostly safest when they hold
a season ticket for the local line.

EVERY LITTLE HELPS
for Paul

Whenever you returned, pockets stuffed with envelopes,
it wasn't the fact of our neighbours' generosity
(though they were ... considering your Third World pitch
had followed on from Age Concern and Save the Children)
nor their sociability (it took you two and a half hours
to cover No. 44 to No. 88, even numbers only) ...
What warmed my heart, and will for weeks to come,
was your throwaway addendum: *As far as I can see,
other peoples' halls are just as cluttered as ours.*

AFTERWARDS
after Hardy

When I'm gone—when they gather round and see the grey
Gradation up the curtains, the mugs' brown rings,
The dust, the clutter, the tacky vinyl—will the neighbours say
'She was a woman who never noticed such things'?

ROUND ABOUT CHRISTMAS EVE

I'm preening the poinsettia
by candlelight. As if there weren't umpteen
gifts to wrap and surfaces to clean,

I'm tuning into Christmas with Sinatra
and teasing red from underneath the green.
I'm preening the poinsettia.

It's like smoothing out the pages of a letter
so every last endearment can be seen
and lingered over—like this in-between
of preening the poinsettia.

WINTER REVISIONS
for Sally Wheeler

When freezing fog evaporates,
the pristine rime that lingers on
brings out photographers, while gardeners
bide their time and watch the lawn ...

Blade by blade the sun prescribes
(more insinuation than decree)
the setting for a garden bench
and where to plant the apple tree.

SPRING

It spills from sun-shocked evenings in March
and slit seed-packets, buckled into spouts.
She palms and strokes and shunts them, via heart-line;
index-fingers them to rows of labelled pots.

They germinate too soon, of course, too soon
a forest of green pins excites the kitchen.
From there, it's nightly shuffles to the greenhouse
and freezing hands that reek of paraffin.

When light allows, she separates each seedling
—barely gripped by thumb and fingertip.
She teases root from root and then re-anchors
their tresses of translucent brittle silks.

The longest month of all is fickle April:
whittled down to digging-weeding days
of riddling soil and fretting over bindweed.
How old, she thinks, her hands become, clay-crazed.

Some afternoon in May, the planting over,
she walks the garden, dazed by sudden heat.
She lifts her head and stares at the horizon
as if awakening to some old grief ...

Don't ask her about daffodils or tulips,
or whether lilac bloomed. She won't have seen
the Honesty that flared in neighbours' gardens
nor the tentative new growth on evergreens.

Have pity on her. Now that June's arrived,
there's sadness in a weather-beaten dreamer
who sleepwalks with her hands outstretched. She's spent
the better part of spring divining summer.

BACKSPIN

Mid-'60s ... Nine or ten I would've been;
snug in the back seat of a Ford Prefect
coasting home from the Sunday run (Warrenpoint)
summer-bare legs bonded to leatherette
and just as we hit Newry Town
—mudflats to the left, gasworks to the right
(more than a hint of the primordial soup
when I think on it now)—
just as we clipped that semi-permanent pothole,
I had a sudden notion of infinity
that filled my head or emptied it.
I can't remember which; can't remember
the notion; what's etched is how
the pleasure of the moment left me goosebumped,
hugging the memory of it ... something like
the rainbow embarkation point of love
—you can't get under it, you can't dissect it,
you just accept it as the bridge from rain to sun ...
all of which makes me think:
I don't sit in the back seat
half enough these days.

KNITTING
for Stephen and Katherine

Even now, thirty years on,
the very mention of No. 8s and 4-ply wool
hauls me back to P5 Needlework
and long, long afternoons in Newry Model School.

Always the unfinished penguin comes to mind.
I never made it out of monochrome
to the yellow beak and feet
or the multicoloured shredded foam

for stuffing. I can feel it yet—
the anxiety; the awful hopelessness;
turning around to Diane Bradley, begging;
and the little breast-piece, worried into grubbiness.

You can't be good at everything.
That's what I tell them, Stevie and Kate,
as they fret the night before Handicraft
and it begins to look like a family trait

although Granny is able and willing.
I wear it like a badge of courage now:
I CAN'T CAST ON—a sort of defiance.
But I'm inclined to think, somehow,

that casting *off* was the real sticking point;
a kind of steel-tipped deferral;
never wanting the whole thing sewn up.
The kids must think I'm a bit of a rebel

the way I just sit scribbling, feet on the pedal-bin,
between the fridge and the back door
—minding the spuds and the grill
or maybe not. They know the score—

the radio on full tilt; the blue fug;
Bleep Bleep Bleep; She's done it again!
and me, flapping at the smoke-alarm
with the *Radio Times*; profane

but laughing along with them. And there I sit—
spinning a yarn that's only half the story.
Though looking back, I can't honestly remember
any particular fondness for poetry ...

LINES
Roseville, Summer 1964

The billhooked laurel hedge.
The narrow border. 'Ena Harkness',
lobelia, alyssum, marigold, 'Peace',
lobelia, alyssum, marigold, 'Iceberg',
lobelia, alyssum, marigold, 'Superstar' ...
The spade-edged lawn. The garden seat
(newly glossy in Buckingham Green)
and Uncle Bertie in his RAF uniform
exhaling, through the Woodbine smoke,
Isn't it fierce about Jim Reeves.

SHORELINE

The breakers of heartache subside
in rarified rockpools. We hide
until shadows grow long
or an old Jim Reeves song
pulls it back. *The remembering tide* ...

SUMMER LOVE WAS EVER THUS ...

like roadside grasses, feathered into bloom,
recoiling from the strangeness of a car
but lunging at its wake—those hapless plumes
seed constellations in the melting tar.

THE UNRELIABLE NARRATOR

Tight-lipped on love, she talks us through a garden
lamenting winter losses; cruel springs;
the weevil-eaten leaves of rhododendron;
the cut-and-come-again of nettle-stings.

But something in the way she handles petals
—smoothing creases, tracing iris falls—
appears to contradict ... And when she stalls
at Rosa *damascena*; when she nuzzles

each full-blown bloom, it goes against the slant
of chill and loneliness that she professes.
Between the Latin names we catch the scent
of someone else—their open lingual kisses.

DANGEROUS DRIVING

I clocked up 60,000 miles
during your years away
in the city of cyclists;
miles as empty as oceans,
knowing that around no corner
across no central reservation
could I glimpse you driving
that modest little hatchback.

You called one day and said
I'm home, I'll get in touch.
You only lingered long enough
to show me your new car—
updated modest little hatchback;
deeper shade of blue.
Take care and call me soon
was all that I could manage.
I watched you drive off
into weeks and months,
God help me, years of no word.

I know that I should ring or write
but phones are lightning conductors;
and the sudden desperation of a letter,
like overtaking on a bend,
is more than I dare ...

You live on my side of town. Your house
is in a cul-de-sac (off a cul-de-sac)
with a bitch of a turning circle
that makes epics of arrivals.
So I trawl the suburbs
never finding fifth gear;
never needing full beam.

How dangerous my driving has become
since your return. By day I scan for indigo.
By night I filter numberplates
sideswiped from the dazzle.
A sticky clutch and dicey brakes say
it's time to trade in. But I'm afraid to.

I'm holding out for the day
that you might drive toward me,
unseen, out of a blinding evening sun;
that you might recognize
this now rare battered saloon
—that you might remember ...

My dear, we are closing on the hour
when we will meet, fatherless,
at the crossroads of the cemetery.
There, in an awkward clinch of grief,
we will know—you and I—
how prodigal we've been
with miles and years.

A LITTLE KNOWLEDGE

You'll arrive out of an April blue
and find me loss-assessing
—sifting through a garden
smug with dandelions. You'll say
*I'm leaving soon ... a change of scene
... new country ... new research.*

I'll go all technical and bluff my way
around the *Brain-Gut Axis*,
Feedback and *Appetite Control*;
and I'll be keen to hear
where your new lab stands re
that Holy Grail, *The Satiety Factor*.

Though what I'll really want to say is
Bugger satiety. What about hunger?
knowing full well how indecently
close they lie in the hypothalamus
—almost touching.

I'll be casually leaning against
the porch wall, arms tightly folded.
You'll be on the lower step,
hands stifled in pockets.
My gaze will drift towards
a clutch of stricken foliage,
more brown than green—vestigial
beside the daffodils.
As conversation dies
I'll trust my eyes to say
*To have begged you to stay
would have been as risky
as overwintering Penstemons.*

WHY?

Some people are just like the moon,
forever waxing and waning; operating
on a different time scale so that
See you tomorrow night, same time,
same place ... never quite comes off.
You lose sight of them for days or weeks.
Mostly, you feel it was something you said
as opposed to something you didn't say.
And you can't help but think of them
lighting up somebody else's life.
So you sit by the window and wait—
afraid to go looking; never quite getting
the whole story. But if you love them
(Why do you *always* love them?)
you forgive their migratory ways.
You forgive them anything, really.

FUCHSIA *MAGELLANICA*
for Carol Rumens

Hardiest of fuchsias, yet in winter,
how brutally you die away to sticks.
No tempered fall; the first November frost
is cautery—melts leaf to cicatrix.

What hormone flux, what angle of the season
tempts you back? You're tentative at first
—just tips of leaves; but soon a rage of sap
that builds till parchment skin begins to burst.

A spate of leaf does well to hide the lesions
that sunlight renders to a flayed maroon.
It's such a purple recklessness that finds you
wreathed in slender flowers by early June.

You tower above those gaudy hot-house sisters
whose fleshy blooms are stiff with counterfeit.
Their year-to-year survival is the whim
of men with knives and fungicide and grit.

It's with a kind of poignance that you bloom
so distant from that South Atlantic shore
where hummingbirds would flatter for your nectar.
Do you miss them? Do you miss the tidal roar?

Yet here you are—as big as Buddleia;
as deeply anchored in this heavy loam.
Fuchsia *magellanica*, concede that this
most temperate of climates could be home.

ALWAYS

Even after the narrative dwindles
(as it will, it surely will) there'll be
elaborations and enumerations:
the odd avalanche of sky-detail;
March's headcount of magnolia buds
and later, wind-corralled against red brick,
the autumn-bruckle chestnut leaves;
their hoard of spiny apples—still intact?
Or scuffled down to shells? For seasons being
not wholly reliable indices
there'll always be some or other pageant
to report—something heartfelt, extant.

ON GOING WITHOUT SAYING

I can't begin to tell you
(I keep *meaning* to tell you)
how it feels to drive away ...
the absolute gobsmackery
of wheeling round the corner
to that face-to-face encounter
with Venus—always there these nights,
completely unfazed by streetlights.
I keep forgetting to mention
this localized phenomenon.
I always happen on it too late—
at the wrong end of your one-way street.
By then, there's no turning back.
But some night, I will. I'll shock
the gearbox into reverse
and drag you out to see Venus.
We'll stand there, basking in irony
—shortsighted-you and stargazer-me.
We'll talk about more than the weather;
and maybe, so lit, I'll remember
what it was I wanted to say,
something relating to constancy ...
But just for now, here I sit,
stoically inarticulate.

AT A BEND IN THE ROAD

Between the church and the River Walk
the bare thorn hedge admits
its weaknesses in barbed wire stitches
and brambles that resolutely arc

from root to rooting tip, finessing
tired mud-spattered nettles
and skeletons of horsetails.
Across the road, north-facing,

the dry-stone wall has little to declare
but winter's coinage of mosses and lichens.
Its few precocious Hart's Tongue ferns
are suddenly gawky in over-exposure.

***

And so, the off-peak tourist,
aslither in the rutted glaur
with no bouquets nor fruits to gather,
is left imagining what's passed

and what's to come: a hedge's
bloom—its staggered shows
of off-white elementary flowers;
its haws and black sweetnesses.

And from a shady wall, rosettes
of primrose leaves, crisp and crimped;
and surely, by degrees, serrated
heart-shaped leaves of violets.

A WATERY CITY
Cork, June 1996

Well if I'd known how many bridges there were in that city
I'd have worried for your soul and I'd never have written
Hope the prose is flowing as effortlessly as the Lee
if I'd considered the sea. I hadn't reckoned on reversible rivers.

But there you were, moon-attuned and berthed between bridges
—girder bridges and carboniferous limestone bridges
stapling street to street. We walked them all, that afternoon
or so it seemed; admired the cheery pastel housefronts,
and grander, bare facades of limestone with an occasional
blush of pink sandstone. We even eyed up steeples
and one particularly incongruous church roof. The plants
were wonderful of course. I knew they would be—
so many tender shrubs in bloom. But the weeds
(old walls alive with clematis and toadflax
—even the *weeds* were exotic) made me realise
just how far I'd come.
        Then something happened.

We had food, I think; some poetry; some drink
and then (this bit's quite strange) a mist came down
and (weirder) we were suddenly afloat.
(Where did that boat come from anyway?)
And just as quick, the sky turned cobalt blue.
The swell was worrying, but oh the view.
All the *Physical Geography of Coasts* I ever knew
came crashing back. Promontories. Arches. Stacks.
There were cliffs on either side, rough-hewn and veined
with schisty glitter. It was some kind of narrows,
but where was it? We scoured the map (the tourist one
you'd lent me, just in case ...) and saw, almost off the edge
and barely legible, as reticent as contour lines—*Desire Straits*.
Alone and oarless, not a buoy in sight, we drifted
mercifully past the rocks towards a crescent beach.

We both managed to graze something or other
clambering out in the shallows. But glad, we were,
of land: a south-facing strand, ripple-creased
and etched with sandpiper scribbles; studded
with shells and tiny stones around the water-line;
and further back—beyond seaweed and bleached branches—
diving underground at rocks and peripheral shingle.
We separated, each to our own surveys—as if expert
in geology et cetera (the books were all at home).
There were doom-black rocks, epic with lichens.
You headed straight for those. I hunkered down
among the fleshy sunset tints of cowrie shells.
An hour passed, or maybe two, before the rendevous
—a huge 'tabletop' of red granite solidly propped
on three short pillars of basalt. I pronounced it an 'erratic'.
You preferred to think of it as a squat dolmen.
Anyway, we emptied our pockets of shells and putative fossils
and as-yet-unnamed wild flowers in squashed bouquets.
There was some discussion about tinctures ... or was it
plate tectonics? Hunger caught us then, and wonder ...
When to push the boat back out—high tide?
Maps were one thing, tide-tables were something else.
We were clueless. Would time and tide wait for *us*?

That's when I lost the gist (again!)
Those rollers of sliceable mist came back
and blanked the whole thing out; and as it lifted,
I saw that our erratic-cum-squat-dolmen
had darkened and mellowed to mahogany. Somebody
was calling *Time!* You were looking at your watch.
And me? I was wondering, among other things ...
how a whole ocean could have evaporated and why
a non-swimmer like me was suddenly longing for the sea;
lonely for even the slightest glimpse of water.
But then you spoke; and looking down, I saw the ice
melting in the glass, the ice melting ...

A WINDLESS NIGHT IN JUNE, THERE BEING NO STARS

Among the slow motion rustles—the evening flotilla of slugs
emerging from the undergrowth: Clematis 'William Kennet'
engaging itself and the cotoneaster; the seasonal abscissions
(old holly leaves and little apples that cannot be held)
—I'm stationed, like an astronomer scanning for meteors;
I'm waiting (any minute now) to hear just one chipping,
flint or chalk, abandoning its weathered bezel
(the shells and bits of glass will surely be the last to fall
from 1930s pebbledash.) Just one percussive plip of gravity
and then I'll go to bed—part vindicated, part in mourning.